GREAT
AMERICAN
STORIES I

GREAT AMERICAN STORIES I
An ESL/EFL Reader

beginning-intermediate to intermediate levels

C. G. Draper

PRENTICE HALL REGENTS, Englewood Cliffs NJ 07632

Library of Congress Cataloging in Publication Data
DRAPER, C. G.
  Great American stories.

  1. English language—Text-books for foreign
speakers. 2. Readers—1950–   3. Short
stories, American. I. Title.
PE1128.D675 1985   428.6′4   84–17823
ISBN 0–13–363748–4 (v. 1)

Editorial/production supervision and
  interior design: F. Hubert
Cover design: Lundgren Graphics, Ltd.
Manufacturing buyer: Harry P. Baisley

Printed in the United States of America

10

ISBN 0-13-363748-4 01

PRENTICE-HALL INTERNATIONAL, INC., *London*
PRENTICE-HALL OF AUSTRALIA PTY. LIMITED, *Sydney*
EDITORA PRENTICE-HALL DO BRASIL, LTDA., *Rio de Janeiro*
PRENTICE-HALL CANADA INC., *Toronto*
PRENTICE-HALL HISPANOAMERICANA, S.A., *Mexico*
PRENTICE-HALL OF INDIA PRIVATE LIMITED, *New Delhi*
PRENTICE-HALL OF JAPAN, INC., *Tokyo*
PRENTICE-HALL OF SOUTHEAST ASIA PTE. LTD., *Singapore*
WHITEHALL BOOKS LIMITED, *Wellington, New Zealand*

CONTENTS

LOVE OF LIFE, Jack London, *29*

MIGGLES, Bret Harte, *43*

A CUB-PILOT'S EDUCATION, Mark Twain, *61*

THE LADY, OR THE TIGER?
Frank Stockton, *81*

AN OCCURRENCE AT OWL CREEK BRIDGE,
Ambrose Bierce, *97*

TO THE READER

This book starts at the beginning-intermediate level. It ends at the intermediate level. The first story in the book will be easy for you. The stories become more difficult, and the last story is the most difficult. The vocabulary list for the first four stories has 600 words. The list for the last three stories has 1000 words. The longest sentences in the first stories have 10 words. In the last stories, they have 18 words. There is new grammar in each story.

By working on this book, you will improve your

- reading skills
- vocabulary
- knowledge of English grammar
- writing skills

If you work on the book in a class with other students, you will also improve your speaking skills.

These stories were written in a more difficult form by seven of America's most famous writers. You will read about the writers' lives before you read their stories. After each story you will find

- 2 reading skills exercises
- 3 vocabulary and grammar exercises
- 1 writing exercise

Good luck, and good reading!

TO THE
TEACHER

Great American Stories I consists of seven careful adaptations of famous stories by classic American writers, and exercises on each story in reading skills, vocabulary, grammar, and writing.

The book is both graded and progressive—that is, the vocabulary, grammar, and internal structure of the stories increase in difficulty from the first story (which is at the beginning-intermediate level of proficiency) to the last (which is at the intermediate level). Structural, lexical, and sentence-length controls have been used throughout the book. For example, the head-word list for the first four stories contains 600 words, while that used for the final three contains 1000; maximum sentence length increases from 10 words in the first story to 18 in the last; and new grammatical structures are added story by story. Words from outside the head-word lists are introduced in a context that helps make their meaning clear; they are used again within the next 100 words of text, and then repeated at least three more times before the end of the story.

The book as a whole is designed to be incorporated into a 10–12 week course in ESL or EFL as part of the reading program. The materials can be used either in or out of class for pleasure reading, controlled discussion, vocabulary development, grammar reinforcement, writing practice, and of course the acquisition of reading skills.

The exercises are so designed that the student must often return to the text to check comprehension, grammar models, or vocabulary points. Further, each story is preceded by a brief biographical paragraph about the story's author; and the first reading skills exercise following the story (an exercise in skimming or scanning) often focuses the reader's attention on that paragraph. In short, a main objective of the book is to involve the reader deeply in the text of each story, and, toward that end, to present exercises that are difficult if not impossible to complete without a thorough understanding of the text.

An answer key to the exercises is available from the publisher, Prentice-Hall, Inc., Englewood Cliffs, NJ 07632.

C. G. D.

GREAT
AMERICAN
STORIES I

THE GIFT
OF THE MAGI

adapted from the story by

O. Henry

O. Henry's real name was William Sydney Porter. He was born in Greensboro, North Carolina, in 1862. He left school at the age of fifteen and worked in many different places. He also spent three years in prison because he took money from a bank. He started to write stories while he was in prison. O. Henry is famous for his stories with surprise endings. "The Gift of the Magi" is perhaps his most famous story. It is from the book *The Four Million,* stories about the everyday people of New York City. O. Henry died in 1910.

Della counted her money three times. She had only one dollar and eighty-seven cents. That was all. And tomorrow would be Christmas. What Christmas gift could she buy with only one dollar and eighty-seven cents? Della lay down on the old bed and cried and cried.

Let's leave Della alone for a while and look at her home. The chairs and tables were old and poor. Outside there was a mailbox without mail, and a door without a doorbell. The name on the door said MR. JAMES DIL- LINGHAM YOUNG—Della's dear husband Jim.

Della knew that Jim would be home soon. She dried her eyes and stood up. She looked in the mirror. She began to comb her hair for Jim. She felt very sad. She wanted to buy Jim a Christmas gift—something good. But what could she do with one dollar and eighty-seven cents? She combed her hair in the mirror and thought. Suddenly she had an idea.

Now, Jim and Della had only two treasures. One was Jim's gold watch. The other was Della's hair. It was long and brown, and fell down her back. Della looked in the mirror a little longer. Her eyes were sad, but then she smiled. She put on her old brown coat and her hat. She ran out of the house and down the street. She stopped in front of a door which said, MME. SOPHRONIE. HAIR OF ALL KINDS. Madame Sophronie was fat and seemed too white. The store was dark.

"Will you buy my hair?" Della asked.

"I buy hair," said Madame. "Take off your hat. Let's see your hair."

Della's hair fell down like water. Mme. Sophronie lift-

ed Della's hair with a heavy hand. "Twenty dollars," she said.

"Give me the money now!" said Della.

Ah! the next two hours flew past like summer wind. Della shopped in many stores for the right gift for Jim. Then she found it—a chain for his gold watch. It was a good chain, strong and expensive. Della knew the chain would make Jim happy. Jim had a cheap chain for his watch, but this chain was much better. It would look good with the gold watch. The chain cost twenty-one dollars. Della paid for the chain, and ran home with eighty-seven cents.

At seven o'clock Della made coffee and started to cook dinner. It was almost dinner time. Jim would be home soon. He was never late. Della heard Jim outside. She looked in the mirror again. "Oh! I hope Jim doesn't kill me!" Della smiled, but her eyes were wet. "But what could I do with only one dollar and eighty-seven cents?"

The door opened, and Jim came in and shut it. His face was thin and quiet. His coat was old, and he had no hat. He was only twenty-two. Jim stood still and looked at Della. He didn't speak. His eyes were strange. Della suddenly felt afraid. She did not understand him. She began to talk very fast. "Oh, Jim, dear, why do you look so strange? Don't look at me like that. I cut my hair and sold it. I wanted to buy you a Christmas gift. It will grow again—don't be angry. My hair grows very fast. Say 'Merry Christmas,' dear, and let's be happy. You don't know what I've got for you—it's beautiful."

"You cut your hair?" Jim spoke slowly.

"I cut it and sold it," Della answered. "Don't you like me now? I'm still me, aren't I?"

"You say that your hair is gone?" Jim asked again.

"Don't look for it, it's gone," Della said. "Be good to me, because it's Christmas. Shall we have dinner now, Jim?"

Jim seemed to wake up. He smiled. He took Della in his arms.

Let us leave them together for a while. They are happy, rich or poor. Do you know about the magi? The magi were wise men who brought Christmas gifts to the baby

Jesus. But they could not give gifts like Jim's and Della's. Perhaps you don't understand me now. But you will understand soon.

Jim took a small box out of his pocket. "I love your short hair, Della," he said. "I'm sorry I seemed strange. But if you open the box you will understand." Della opened the box. First she smiled, then suddenly she began to cry. In the box were two beautiful combs. Combs like those were made

to hold up long hair. Della could see that the combs came from an expensive store. She never thought she would have anything as beautiful! "Oh, Jim, they are beautiful! And my hair grows fast, you know. But wait! You must see your gift." Della gave Jim the chain. The chain was bright, like her eyes. "Isn't it a good one, Jim? I looked for it everywhere. You'll have to look at the time one hundred times daily, now. Give me your watch. I want to see them together."

Jim lay back on the bed. He put his hands under his head, and smiled. "Della," he said, "let's put the gifts away. They are too good for us right now. I sold the watch to buy your combs. Come on, let's have dinner."

The magi, as we said, were wise men—very wise men. They brought gifts to the baby Jesus. The magi were wise, so their gifts were wise gifts. Perhaps Jim and Della do not seem wise. They lost the two great treasures of their house. But I want to tell you that they *were* wise. People like Jim and Della are always wiser than others. Everywhere they are wiser. They are the magi.

E X E R C I S E S

A. Reading Skill: Scanning

Read the questions below. The answer to each question can be found in the paragraph about O. Henry on p. 1. Read the paragraph quickly, looking for the piece of information that will answer each question. You do not need to understand everything in the paragraph. But you must read carefully enough to find the answer to each question. This kind of reading to find information is called *scanning*.

1. In what town was O. Henry born?
2. How old was he when he left school?
3. Why did he spend time in prison?
4. What is O. Henry famous for?
5. What is *The Four Million?*
6. How old was O. Henry when he died?

B. Reading Skill: Understanding the Main Ideas

Answer the following questions with complete sentences.

1. Why did Della want to buy a gift for Jim?
2. How do you know that Della and Jim were not rich?
3. What were Jim's and Della's greatest treasures?
4. How did Della get enough money for Jim's gift?
5. How did Jim get enough money for Della's gift?
6. Who were the magi, and what did they do?
7. Why does the writer think Della and Jim were wise?

C. Word Order

The words in the sentences below are in the wrong order.
Put them in the right order.

Example:

her money counted three times Della.
Della counted her money three times.

1. put on Della coat and hat her old brown.

2. Della's hair with a heavy hand lifted Mme. Sophronie.

3. and ran home Della the chain paid for.

4. smiled Della were wet her eyes but.

5. home would for dinner be Jim soon.

6. Della's combs Jim the watch to buy sold.

7. was like Della's eyes bright the chain.

D. Verb Forms:
will / would and *can / could*

Choose the correct form of the verb *will / would* or *can /
could* in the following sentences.

Example:

I had no money. I (can / could) _____*could*_____ not
buy a gift.

1. Della wanted to buy Jim a present because the next day (will / would) _____ be Christmas.

2. She saved her money for many months. But what (can / could) _____ she buy with only one dollar and eighty-seven cents?

3. The chain was expensive. Della knew it (will / would) _____ make Jim happy.

4. Jim said, "If you open the box, you (will / would) _____ understand why I seem strange."

5. "We (can't / couldn't) _____ use our gifts right now," Jim said.

E. Vocabulary

For each empty space in the sentences below, choose the best word from the following list:

merry	watch	wise	doorbell
mirror	gift	count	

1. It is not possible to _____ the stars.

2. People are often _____ at parties.

3. Is John in love with himself? When he stands near a _____, he always looks into it.

4. "You don't need a lot of money to give the

_____ of yourself," the old man said.

5. He didn't want to be late for the bus, so he looked at his

_____ almost every minute.

6. No one answered the _____. Perhaps they

were sleeping, or they weren't at home.

7. It is not _____ for a poor man to throw

eggs at a king.

F. Writing:
Madame Sophronie Speaks

In this exercise, you are Madame Sophronie. Answer each
question below. Use complete sentences. When there are
two questions together, join your answers using the words
in parentheses.

Example:

What is your name? Do you have a store in the city, or in
the country? (*and*)

My name is Madame Sophronie, and I have a store in the
city.

1. Do you buy hair, or do you buy gold chains? Do you sell
   hair, too, or don't you? (*and*)

2. One day, did a young woman come into your store, or was
   it her husband?

3. Did she want to sell her hair or to buy it? Did you tell her to take her hat off, or to put it on?   (*and*)

4. Was her hair beautiful, or ugly? Did you tell her that, or not?   (*but*)

5. How much did you tell her you would pay?

6. Did she need the money, or didn't she? Did she take it, or not?   (*so*)

7. Did you take her money, or did you take her hair? Did you want to buy it later, or sell it later?   (*because*)

After you have answered the questions above, put your seven answers together into one paragraph. Then add to it another paragraph, about this:

Then a rich woman came into your store. She wanted to buy some hair. What did she say to you? What did you say to her? Did you show her the young woman's beautiful hair? Did she like it? How much did she pay for it?

THE
TELL-TALE
HEART

adapted from the story by

Edgar Allan Poe

Edgar Allan Poe was born in 1809 in Boston, Massachusetts. He is one of America's most important and famous writers. Poe's parents died when he was a child. He was raised by people named Allan. They were rich, but Poe was poor all his life. He lost several jobs because he drank too much. People remember Poe for his poetry, for his detective stories, and for his horror stories like "The Tell-Tale Heart." Poe died unhappily at the age of forty, in 1849.

Before you read this story, do Exercise A on p. 21.

True! Nervous. I was nervous then and I am nervous now. But why do you say that I am mad? Nothing was wrong with me. I could see very well. I could smell. I could touch. Yes, my friend, and I could hear. I could hear all things in the skies and in the earth. So why do you think that I am mad? Listen. I will tell you the story. I will speak quietly. You will understand everything. Listen!

Why did I want to kill the old man? Ah, this is very difficult. I liked the old man. No, I loved him! He never hurt me. He was always kind to me. I didn't need his gold; no, I didn't want that. I think it was his eye—yes, it was this! He had the eye of a bird. It was a cold, light-blue eye—a horrible eye. I feared it. Sometimes I tried to look at it. But then my blood ran cold. So, after many weeks, I knew I must kill the old man. His horrible eye must not live. Do you understand?

Now here is the point. You think that I am mad. Madmen know nothing. But I? I was careful. Oh, I was very careful. *Careful,* you see? For one long week, I was very kind to the old man. But every night, at midnight, I opened his door slowly, carefully. I had a lantern with me. Inside the lantern there was a light. But the sides of the lantern hid the light. So, first I put the dark lantern through the open door. Then I put my head in the room. I put it in slowly, very slowly. I didn't want to wake the old man. Ha! Would a madman be careful, like that? There was no noise, not a sound. I opened the lantern carefully—very care-

fully—and slowly. A thin light fell upon the old man's eye. I held it there. I held it there for a long time. And I did this every night for seven nights. But always the eye was closed. And so I could not do my work. I was not angry at the old man, you see. I was angry only at his horrible eye. And every morning I went into his room happily. I was friendly with him. I asked about his night. Did he sleep well? Was he all right? And so, you see, he knew nothing.

On the eighth night, I was more careful than before. I know you don't believe me, but it is true. The clock's hand moved more quickly than my hand. I opened the door slowly. I put the lantern in the room. The old man moved suddenly in his bed. But I did not go back. The room was very dark. I knew he could not see me. I put my head in the room. I began to open the lantern, but my hand hit the side. It made a loud noise.

The old man sat up quickly in bed. "Who's there?" he cried.

I stood still and said nothing. For one long hour I did not move a finger. And he did not lie down. He sat in his bed. He listened. I knew his fear!

And soon I heard another sound. It came from the old man. It was a horrible sound, the sound of fear! I knew that sound well. Often, at night, I too have made that sound. What was in the room? The old man didn't know. He didn't want to know. But he knew that he was in danger. Ah, yes, he knew!

And now I began to open the lantern. I opened it just a little. A small thin light fell upon the horrible blue eye.

It was open—wide, wide open. I could not see the old man's face or body. But I saw the eye very well. The horrible bird's eye. My blood ran cold. At the same time, anger began to grow inside me.

And now, haven't I told you that I could hear everything? Now a low, quick sound came to my ears. It was like

the sound of a small wooden clock. I knew *that* sound well, too. It was the beating of the old man's heart!

My fear and anger grew. But I did not move. I stood still. I held the light on the old man's eye. And the beating of the heart grew. It became quicker and quicker, and louder and louder every second! I knew that his fear was very great. *Louder,* do you hear? I have told you that I am nervous. And this is true. My fear was like the old man's. But I did not move. I held the light on his eye. But the beating grew louder, LOUDER! And now a new fear came to me. Someone in the next house would hear! The old man must die! This was his hour! With a loud cry, I opened the lantern wide. I ran into the room! The old man cried loudly once—once only. His fear, his fear killed him! In a second I pulled him from the bed. He lay still. I smiled a little. Everything was all right. For some minutes, I heard his heart beat softly. Then it stopped. I put my hand on his body. He was cold. He was like a stone. The old man was dead. His eye would never look upon me again!

And now I was very, very careful. I worked quickly but quietly. I used a good, new knife. I cut off the old man's arms and legs and head. Then I took three boards from the floor of the room. I put everything below the floor. Then I put the boards in their place again. I cleaned the floor. There was no blood. Nothing was wrong. I was *careful,* you see? Ha! Can you still think that I am mad?

I finished. It was four o'clock—still dark as midnight. Suddenly there was a beating on the door. Someone was there. But I went down with a happy heart. I had nothing to fear. Nothing.

Three policemen came into the house. They said that someone in the next house heard a cry. Was something wrong? Was everyone all right?

"Of course," I said. "Please come in." I was not nervous. I smiled at the men. I told them that the old man was

in another town. I said he was with his sister. I showed them his money, his gold. Everything was there, in its place.

I brought chairs. I asked the men to sit. I sat, too. I sat on the boards over the dead man's body! I talked easily. The policemen smiled.

But after some minutes I became tired. Perhaps I was a little nervous. There was a low sound in my head, in my ears. I didn't like it. I talked more loudly, more angrily. Then suddenly I understood. The sound was not in my head or in my ears. It was there in the room!

Now I know that I became *very* nervous. *It was a low quick sound. It sounded like a small wooden clock!* My eyes opened wide. Could the policemen hear it? I talked in a louder voice. But the noise did not stop. It grew! I stood up and talked angrily, dangerously. I walked across the floor and back again. Why wouldn't the men leave? There was a storm inside my head! And still the noise became louder— LOUDER—LOUDER! I beat my hands on the table. I said dangerous things in a loud voice. But still the men talked happily and smiled. Couldn't they hear? Was it possible? Oh, God! No, no! They heard! They knew! They laughed at my hopes, and smiled at my fears. I knew it then and I know it now. I couldn't keep still! Anything was better than their smiles and laughing! And now—again!—listen! louder! LOUDER! LOUDER!

"Stop!" I cried. "Enough! Enough! Pull up the boards! Below the floor! Here, here!—It is the beating of his horrible heart!"

E X E R C I S E S

A. Reading Skill: Skimming

Sometimes we want to have a general idea about a piece of writing before we read it carefully. This exercise will show you one way of doing that.

Quickly read the first two sentences of each paragraph in "The Tell-Tale Heart." Do not read more than that. This kind of fast reading is called *skimming*. After you skim the story, do not look back at it again, but do the following exercise immediately.

Which of the words below do you remember reading? Underline the words that you remember.

nervous	beautiful	careful
guitar	kiss	ice cream
policeman	kill	fear
baby	dark	dance
sunlight	midnight	old man
mad	flowers	happy

Now, on a piece of paper, put the underlined words in one group. Put the other words in another group. What is the difference between the two groups? What do you think happens in the story?

Finally, read the story carefully, and then do Exercise B.

B. Reading Skill:
Understanding Cause and Effect

Complete each sentence below by choosing **a, b,** or **c.** The first half of each sentence tells about something that happened in the story (the *effect*). The second half should tell why it happened (the *cause*).

1. The young man wanted to kill the old man because

    a. he loved the old man.
    b. he didn't like the old man's eye.
    c. he wanted the old man's gold.

2. He opened the old man's door carefully because

    a. the old man was mad.
    b. he thought the old man was horrible.
    c. he didn't want to wake the old man.

3. Every morning, the young man was friendly because he

    a. held a thin light over the old man's eye.
    b. didn't want the old man to think anything was wrong.
    c. was angry at the old man.

4. The police came to the house because

    a. someone in the next house heard a cry.
    b. they knew the young man was mad.
    c. they wanted to sit, talk, and laugh.

5. The young man talked louder and louder to the police because

    a. they couldn't hear him.

   b. he thought they would hear the beating of the old
      man's heart.

   c. he was very angry at them.

6. The young man killed the old man and then told the police because

   a. they all laughed and smiled at him.

   b. the old man's heart beat louder and louder.

   c. the young man was mad.

C. Verb Tense:
Past Irregular

In the following sentences, change the verb into the past
tense. All the verbs in this exercise are irregular.

Example:

I (hold) _____*held*_____ the lantern in my hand.

The sides of the lantern (hide) _____ the

light. I (begin) _____ to open the lantern,

but my hand (hits) _____ the side. It

(makes) _____ a loud noise. The old man

(sits) _____ up quickly in bed. I (stand)

_____ still and (say) _____

nothing. Soon I (hear) _____ another

sound. It (comes) _____ from the old man. I

(know) _____ that sound well. It (is)

_____ the sound of fear. My blood (runs)

_____ cold. The beating of the heart

(grows) _____ louder. But I (hold)

_____ the lantern on his eye. Then I (run)

_____ into the room. Later, I (take)

_____ three boards from the floor. I (put)

_____ everything below the floor. But then

I   (become) _____ nervous. I   (tell)

_____ the police everything.

D. Clauses: Adverbial

For each beginning of a sentence under **A**, choose the correct ending from under **B**.

A	**B**
1. The mad man thought	A. when he heard a low, quick sound
2. He wanted to kill the old man	B. after the young man ran into the room
3. The old man woke up	C. that he could hear all things in the earth and in the sky
4. The old man died	

A	**B**
5. The young man told the police	**D.** when the young man's hand hit the lantern
6. The young man became nervous	**E.** because he was afraid of the beating of the heart below the floor
7. He told the police about the killing	**F.** that the old man was in another town
	G. because he hated his cold blue eye

E. Word Forms: Adjectives and Adverbs

Put the correct form of the word on the left in the blank space in the sentence on the right.

Example:

(slow / slowly) He moved _____*slowly*_____ in the dark room.

1. (horrible / horribly) The old man's eye seemed _____ to the young man.

2. (careful / carefully) The young man opened the lantern _____.

3. (dangerous / dangerously) The young man did not seem _____ to the old man.

4. (quick / quickly) The heart beat _____

like a small wooden clock.

5. (nervous / nervously) He became _____

when he heard the beating of the heart.

6. (angry / angrily) The young man began to talk

_____ to the police.

7. (mad / madly) The young man was _____,

though at first he did not talk _____.

F. Writing:
A Police Report

You are one of the policemen in "The Tell-Tale Heart."
You must write a report about the killing. In your report,
you should answer some or all of the following questions:

What time was it when you went to the young man's
house?

Why did you go there?

Did he meet you at the door?

How did he seem—friendly? nervous? angry?

Did he ask you to come in?

Did you ask about the old man?

What did he say to that?

Where did he take you?

Did he ask you to sit?

Did he sit, too?

How did he talk?

But after some minutes, how did he seem?

How did he talk then?

Finally, what did he say?

What did you find below the boards?

What did it look like?

And what do you think about him now?

What should we do with him?

Should we send him to prison? to a doctor?

Should we put him to death?

LOVE
OF LIFE

adapted from the story by

Jack London

Jack London was born of a poor family in San Francisco, in 1876. He left school at fourteen, and became a sailor, a hunter, and an explorer. His first long trip was to Japan. When he was eighteen he returned to high school for one year. Then he went to the University of California at Berkeley. But again he left after one year, and began to write seriously. In 1897 he went to the Klondike in Canada. Many men went there to find gold. London found adventures that he put into his most famous stories and novels. London continued to travel until a few years before his death in 1916.

Two men walked slowly through the low water of a river. They were alone in the cold empty land. All they could see were stones and earth. It was fall, and the river ran cold over their feet. They carried blankets on their backs. They had guns, but no bullets; matches, but no food.

"I wish we had just two of those bullets we hid in the camp," said the first of the men. His voice was tired. The other man did not answer.

Suddenly the first man fell over a stone. He hurt his foot badly, and he cried out. He lay still for a moment, and then called: "Hey, Bill, I've hurt my foot." Bill didn't stop or look back. He walked out of the river and over the hill. The other man watched him. His eyes seemed like the eyes of a sick animal. He stood up. "Bill!" he cried again. But there was no answer. Bill kept walking.

"Bill!"

The man was alone in the empty land. His hands were cold, and he dropped his gun. He fought with his fear, and took his gun out of the water. He followed slowly after Bill. He tried to walk lightly on his bad foot.

He was alone, but he was not lost. He knew the way to their camp. There he would find food, bullets, and blankets. He must find them soon. Bill would wait for him there. Together they would go south to the Hudson Bay Company. They would find food there, and a warm fire. Home. The man had to believe that Bill would wait for him at the camp. If not, he would die. He thought about the food in the camp. And the food at the Hudson Bay Company. And the food he ate two days ago. He thought about food and he walked. After a while the man found some small berries to eat. The

berries had no taste, and did not fill him. But he knew he must eat them.

In the evening he hit his foot on a stone and fell down. He could not get up again. He lay still for a long time. Later, he felt a little better and got up. He made a fire. He could cook only hot water, but he felt warmer. He dried his shoes by the fire. They had many holes. His feet had blood on them. His foot hurt badly. He put his foot in a piece of his blanket. Then he slept like a dead man.

He woke up because he heard an animal near him. He thought of meat and took his gun. But he had no bullets. The animal ran away. The man stood up and cried out. His foot was much worse this morning. He took out a small bag that was in his blanket. It was heavy—fifteen pounds. He didn't know if he could carry it. But he couldn't leave it behind. He had to take it with him. He had to be strong enough. He put it into his blanket again.

That day his hunger grew worse, worse than the hurt in his foot. Many times he wanted to lie down, but hunger made him go on. He saw a few birds. Once he tried to catch one, but it flew away. He felt tired and sick. He forgot to follow the way to the camp. In the afternoon he found some green plants. He ate them fast, like a horse. He saw a small fish in a river. He tried to catch it with his cup. But the fish swam away into a hole. The man cried like a baby, first quietly, then loudly. He cried alone in that empty world.

That night he made a fire again, and drank hot water. His blanket was wet, and his foot hurt. He could think only of his hunger. He woke up cold and sick. The earth and sky were grey. He got up and walked, he didn't know where. But the small bag was with him. The sun came out again, and he saw that he was lost. Was he too far north? He turned toward the east. His hunger was not so great, but he knew he was sick. He stopped often. He heard wolves, and knew that deer were near him. He believed he had one more bul-

let in his gun. It was still empty. The small bag became too heavy. The man opened the bag. It was full of small pieces of gold. He put half the gold in a piece of his blanket and left it on a rock. But he kept his gun. There were bullets in that camp.

Days passed, days of rain and cold. One day he came to the bones of a deer. There was no meat on the bones. The man knew wolves must be near. He broke the bones and ate like an animal. Would he, too, be only bones tomorrow? And why not? This was life, he thought. Only life hurt. There was no hurt in death. To die was to sleep. Then why was he not ready to die? He could not see or feel. The hunger, too, was gone. But he walked and walked.

One morning he woke up beside a river. Sunlight was warm on his face. A sunny day, he thought. Perhaps he could find his way to the camp. His eyes followed the river. He could see far. The river emptied into the sea. He saw a ship on that silver sea. He shut his eyes. He knew there could be no ship, no seas, in this land. He heard a noise behind him, and turned back. A wolf, old and sick, was following him. I know *this* is real, he thought. He turned again, but the sea and the ship were still there. He didn't understand it. He tried to remember. What did the men at the Hudson Bay Company say about this land? Was he walking north, away from the camp, toward the sea? The man moved slowly toward the ship. He knew the sick wolf was following him. In the afternoon he found more bones left by wolves. The bones of a man! Beside the bones was a small bag of gold, like his own. Ha! Bill carried his gold to the end, he thought. He would take Bill's gold to the ship. He would have the last laugh on Bill. His laughing sounded like the low cry of an animal. The wolf cried back to the man, and the man stopped laughing. How could he laugh about Bill's bones? He could not take Bill's gold. He left the gold near the bones.

The man was very sick, now. He walked more and more slowly. His blanket was gone. He lost his gold, then his gun, then his knife. Only the wolf stayed with him hour after hour. At last the man could go no further. He fell down. The wolf came close to him. It weakly bit his hand. The man hit the wolf and it went away. But it did not go far.

It waited. The man waited. After many hours the wolf came back again. It was going to kill the man. But the man was ready. He held the wolf's mouth closed, and he got on top of the sick wolf. He held the animal still. Then he bit it with his last strength. He tasted the wolf's blood in his mouth. Only love of life gave him enough strength. He held the wolf with his teeth and killed it. Later he fell on his back and slept.

* * *

The men on the ship saw a strange thing on the land. It did not walk. It was lying on the ground, and it moved slowly toward them—perhaps twenty feet an hour. The men went close to look at it. They could not believe it was a man.

Three weeks later the man felt better. He could tell them his story. But there was one strange thing. He could not believe there was enough food on the ship. The men told him there was a lot of food. But he only looked at them with fear. And slowly he began to grow fat. The men thought this was strange. They gave him less food, but still he grew larger and larger—each day he was fatter. Then one day they saw him put a lot of bread under his shirt. They looked in his bed, too, and saw bread under his blanket. The men understood, and left him alone.

EXERCISES

A. Reading Skill:
Scanning

Scan the paragraph about Jack London on p. 29, and find answers to the questions below.

1. In what year did London first leave school?

2. How many years did he spend in college?

3. Why did he leave college?

4. Where is the Klondike?

5. Why did men go there?

6. What are London's most famous stories about?

7. How old was London when he died?

B. Reading Skill: Remembering Important Details

If the sentence is true, write "T" next to it. If it is not true, write "F" for false. If the sentence is false, change one word and make it true.

1. _____ The man could not walk quickly because he hurt his back.

2. _____ The man wanted to find the camp because there was gold in it.

3. _____ One day the man found and ate the bones of a fish.

4. _____ The wolf could not kill the man because the wolf, too, was sick.

5. _____ The man found Bill's gold and Bill's bones.

6. _____ The men on the boat did not take the man's hidden meat.

7. _____ The men on the boat understood why the man was always angry.

C. Prepositions

Choose the best preposition for each empty space in the following sentences.

1. The men hid food, blankets, and bullets _____ (on, in, to) their camp.

2. The man dropped his gun _____ (onto, into, under) the water.

3. The man believed that Bill would wait for him

_____ (at, on, to) the camp.

4. He dried his shoes _____ (in, by, on) the fire.

5. The sunlight was warm _____ (in, at, on) the

man's face _____ (in, at, on) the morning.

6. He turned quickly because he heard a noise

_____ (in front of, behind, above) him.

7. The strange thing on the ground moved slowly

_____ (to, toward, at) the men on the boat.

D. Articles

In the empty spaces in the following sentences, put _a, an, the, some,_ or _X_ (if you think there should be no word).

_____ man thought about _____ food. He

thought about _____ food in _____ camp and

_____ food at _____ Hudson Bay Company. He

found _____ small berries and ate them. But

_____ berries did not fill him. Later he made

_____ fire. He could cook only _____ hot water,

but _____ hot water warmed him. He dried his shoes

by _____ fire. _____ shoes had many holes. His

foot hurt badly. He put _____ foot in _____ piece

of his blanket. The next day, his hunger was worse than

_____ hurt in _____ foot. He found _____ bones, but _____ bones did not have _____ meat on them. Would he, too, be _____ bones tomorrow? And why not? This was _____ life, he thought. Only _____ life hurt. There was no hurt in _____ death.

E. Vocabulary: Matching Words

For each sentence below, choose a word from the following list which best fits the sentence.

Example:

_____*bag*_____ He carried his gold in it.

bag	blanket	hunger	camp
strength	bullet	wolf	bones

1. _____ Once, the man in the story believed he had one but really he knew that he didn't have any.

2. _____ He made pieces of it, one for his hurt foot and another for half of his gold.

3. _____ He thought he could find it, but he didn't.

4. _____ He killed it in the way it would kill him.

5. _____ He ate them, and he thought he might die and become them.

6. _____ He didn't want it, but every day he had more of it.

7. _____ He needed it, but every day he had less of it.

F. Writing:
A Letter Home

You are one of the men on the ship in "Love of Life." Write a letter to your family at home. Tell them the strange story of the man you found.

Where did you find him?

What did he look like on that first day?

Did you think he would live, or not?

On the ship, little by little, what happened to him?

And what was strange about him?

Why did he look at the other men with fear?

One day, what did you see him do?

What did you find in his bed?

Why, then, did you leave him alone?

What do you think will happen to him?

MIGGLES

adapted from the story by

Bret Harte

Bret Harte was born in Albany, New York, in 1837. In 1854, he went to the far West. There he wrote for newspapers. Then he began writing short stories about the West, and these made him famous. Later, he worked for the United States government in Germany and Scotland. He spent his last seventeen years in London, and died in 1902.

Before you read this story, do Exercise A on p. 53.

I

We were eight, with the driver. At the beginning of our ride, there was a lot of talking. But now no one spoke or wanted to speak. The ride was long, the road was bad, and we were tired.

They were all asleep. The Judge, who liked to talk, slept with his mouth open. The tall man next to him slept with his hat on. The French lady was asleep, too, on the back seat. The lady from Virginia slept in her expensive clothes. And her husband slept. Only Yuba Bill, the driver, was awake.

The wheels of the stagecoach were noisy below us. Above us, rain fell loudly on the top of the stagecoach. There were no other sounds.

Suddenly the stagecoach stopped. We heard voices. The driver shouted to someone in the road. The man shouted back, above the storm. "Bridge is gone!" we heard the stranger say. "Twenty feet of water! Can't pass!" There was more shouting, but we couldn't understand the words. Then there was a last shout.

"Try Miggles'".

Slowly, the stagecoach turned. We saw the horses that were in the lead. The stranger, who was on horseback, lifted his hand. Then he was lost in the rain. The stagecoach

started again. It seemed that we were on our way to Miggles'.

But who and where was Miggles? The Judge, who knew the country well, did not remember the name. No one knew anything about Miggles. But we believed we would be all right at Miggles' place. We would be dry.

The road got worse, and wetter. But then we stopped in front of a stone wall. The driver got down. He tried to open the door in the wall. It would not open.

"Miggles! O Miggles!"

No answer.

"Migg-ells! You! Miggles!" shouted the driver. But again there was no answer. The Judge put his head out the window. He asked the driver a lot of questions. But Yuba Bill answered only that we must all call for Miggles. So we did that. Together we shouted through the rain "Miggles! Hey, Miggles!"

And a voice came back to us. "Miggles! Hey, Miggles!" We couldn't believe it.

We shouted again "Miggles! Miggles!"

And the Judge said loudly, "My dear sir, please let us come in! We have women here. Try to understand, sir. It is a bad storm, and. . . ."

"Miggles! Miggles! Miggles!" came the voice. "Ha ha ha ha!"

At this, Yuba Bill became angry. He lifted up a large stone. He threw it at the wall door. The door fell down, and we went inside.

It was dark, but we knew we were in a garden. We walked through the wet flowers. At the end of the garden was a long, wooden house. Yuba Bill opened the door and we went in.

There was a long room. At one end, a fire burned in the fireplace. In front of the fire, someone sat in a large chair.

"Hello," said Yuba Bill. "Are you Miggles?"

The person didn't speak or move. Bill was holding the stagecoach lamp. Now he held the lamp next to the person's face. It was a man's face. He was a young man, but the face looked old. The large eyes went to Bill's face. Then they went to the lamp. They stayed there.

"Miggles!" said Bill. "Can't you hear? Come! You can talk!" He pulled the man's arm. The man almost fell over. We had to lift him and hold him up.

"I . . . I don't understand," said Bill. He moved slowly away from the man who wouldn't move, or couldn't move. "I'll go outside to look. There must be some other person here." He went. The rest of us came closer to the fire.

"Well, now," said the Judge. "My friends, it seems that this young man is ill. We must now ask the question, 'Is he Miggles?'"

"Miggles! Miggles! Miggles!" came a voice. The Judge jumped. We looked around in fear. Then, above the fireplace, we saw a black bird. We laughed. This was the voice we had heard from the road.

Yuba Bill was back in a minute. He said, "No one. There's no one here. Only that man who won't talk. Well, I'll tell you something. He'll talk now. I'll. . . ."

But a noise stopped him. We heard feet running outside. The door opened suddenly. A young woman came into the room. She was tired from running. But she smiled at us: white teeth, dark eyes in a lovely face. She shut the door and put her back against it.

"Oh!" she said. "I'm sorry I was late. I'm Miggles!"

So this was Miggles! This young, bright-eyed woman. She was wet, from her simple but pretty dress to her heavy shoes. She took off her wet hat. Lovely brown hair fell to her shoulders.

"You see, boys," she said, and laughed, perhaps at Yuba Bill's sudden smile. "You see, boys, you passed me on the road, a mile away. I knew you would come here. So I ran

all the way home. No one was here, only Jim, and—well—
here I am!" She laughed again. She put her hat down beside
Yuba Bill. Then she went across the room to the sick man.
She put her hand on his arm and looked in his face. His dark
empty eyes looked back at hers. A little life seemed to come
into his face. Miggles laughed again—she had a beautiful
laugh—and turned to us.

"Um, this—er—ill person is . . ." the Judge began.

"Jim," said Miggles.

"Your father?"

"No."

"Brother?"

"No."

"Husband?"

Miggles looked quickly at the two ladies. Then she
said, "No. It's just Jim."

II

For a minute no one spoke. The French Lady and the rich
lady from Virginia City moved closer together.

Miggles smiled. "Well, who will help me with dinner?"
she said. All the men quickly moved to help her.

The meal was simple: coffee, bread, some meat. But it
was a happy meal, full of laughter. Miggles made it happy.
And then, in the middle of the meal, we heard a strange
noise. It sounded like a heavy body which moved against
the outside walls. Then it was at the door.

"That's Joaquin," said Miggles. "Would you like to see
him?" She quickly went and opened the door. Outside, in
the rain, was a big brown bear! It was a wild bear, but it
seemed to know Miggles. It suddenly stood up on two legs
like a man. It held its front legs out to the room. The two
ladies cried out.

"Oh, he doesn't eat people," Miggles told them. "Well, he doesn't eat *friends*. He keeps me out of danger," she said. She fed something to the bear. Then she closed the door.

Again, for a moment, no one spoke. A woman like Miggles was something new to us. She lived with a sick man who was not her husband. But she was happy. She was alone in the wide world. But she was not afraid. The chairs in her house were only boxes. The pictures on her walls were from newspapers. But everything had the touch of a woman. She could talk like a man, and she kept a wild bear. But she was more beautiful than the soft French lady or the rich lady from Virginia City.

Because of all this, the two ladies did not like her very much. And Miggles seemed to know it. After dinner, she quickly showed them to their bed in the other room.

She was gone from the big room for a short time. In that time, we men talked about her. We put our heads together and talked in low voices. We smiled and asked questions, and laughed at the answers. We talked quickly, all together at the same time. People say that only old women talk like that. People are wrong.

In the middle of our talk, Miggles came back. She had a heavy coat over one arm. She seemed strangely quiet, perhaps sad. She pulled a chair over to the sick man, and sat down. "If it's all right with you, I'll stay here tonight," she said. She put the coat around her body. She took the man's hand in hers. She turned her eyes to the fire, and was quiet. None of us spoke. The rain fell all around. The wind cried outside.

Suddenly she looked up at us.

"Is there any of you that knows me?"

There was no answer.

"Think again! I lived in Marysville in '53. Everybody knew me there. I owned the Polka Bar. You understand? Drinking men were my business, boys. People said I was wild. That was before I came to live with Jim. Six years ago. Perhaps I *was* wild. Perhaps I've changed."

She turned her face to the fire. None of us knew what to say, so we said nothing. Slowly, the rest of her story came out.

"It was like this," she said. "Jim here knew me well. He spent a lot of money at my bar. He spent a lot of money on me. I think he spent all he had. Then one day he came into my back room. He sat down on my best chair, like you see him now. And he never moved again without help. No one knew a name for his illness. The doctors thought he would die soon. Or they said he would be a baby all his life. They said I should send him away. But I said 'No.' And why? Perhaps it was something in Jim's eyes. Perhaps it was that I never had a baby. Well, I sold my business and bought this old place. And I brought my baby here."

The body of the quiet man was between Miggles and us. It could say nothing. But it seemed to tell a sad story of love.

"People here are kind," Miggles said. "They don't visit often. In the beginning, it was difficult. My old life was full of laughter and games. Now, I was very alone. But then I found Joaquin, the bear, in the woods. Another baby, but a growing baby! And then there's Polly. She's the bird you met earlier. She knows all kinds of games. And Jim here," said Miggles, with her old laugh. "Jim—why, boys, he knows a *lot* for a man like him. Sometimes I bring him flowers, and I tell you he *knows* them. You can see it in his eyes."

"Why," asked the Judge, "don't you marry this man? You've given him all your young life."

"Well," said Miggles slowly, "I live with Jim because I want to. Not because I have to. I don't want that to change."

"But you are still young, still beautiful. . . ."

"It's getting late," she said softly. "You will all want to

get some sleep. Good night, boys." Miggles pulled her coat around her. She lay down beside Jim's chair, her head near his feet. The fire slowly went down in the fireplace. We, too, lay down on the floor. Soon there was no sound but the rain outside, and the sounds of sleeping.

In the morning, there was coffee on the table, but Miggles was gone. We looked around the house. We waited by the stagecoach. But she did not come back. It seemed she did not like goodbyes.

But on the road, a long way away, we saw her. She stood on a little hill. Her hair flew in the wind. Her teeth, her smile, her eyes were bright. She lifted a hand to us, and we lifted our hats and shouted. Then we went on our way, without speaking, lost in thought. We arrived later at a resting place which had a bar. Then, the Judge leading, we walked inside. We took our places at the bar.

"Are your glasses full, men?" asked the Judge.

They were.

"Well, then. Let's drink to Miggles!" he said, and lifted his glass. "And let's hope that life brings her everything she wants!"

But perhaps she had that already. Who knows?

E X E R C I S E S

A. Reading Skill:
Skimming for Specific Information

Sometimes we need to skim a story or essay to find one or two pieces of information. We don't need to read everything. We don't even need a general idea about the story. We need to remember only the information that we find.

We do this by reading very quickly. Our eyes move rapidly across and down the page, looking for a single word, or perhaps a number. When we find this word or number, we stop and read more carefully. When we find the information we need, we stop reading.

In this exercise, you will try to answer the questions below by skimming a page of the story "Miggles". The answer to each question can be found on the page given. In each question, a name or number has been underlined. Let your eyes move rapidly across and down the page. When they find the underlined name or number, stop. Read more carefully, and find the answer to the question. Try to answer each question in 30 seconds or less.

1. p. 44. Was <u>Yuba Bill</u> a driver, or a judge?

2. p. 47. Was <u>Miggles</u> a man, or a woman?

3. p. 49. Was <u>Joaquin</u> a lawyer, or a bear?

4. p. 50. Where did Miggles live in '53?

5. p. 50. Who owned the Polka Bar?

6. p. 51. Who was Polly?

Note: Exercises B and C are about Part I (pp. 44–49).

B. Reading Skill: Remembering Important Events

Finish the following sentences, using information from the story.

Example:

The sounds in the stagecoach came from

The sounds in the stagecoach came from the wheels under the stagecoach and the rain on top.

1. The stagecoach had to stop because

2. At the stone wall, the driver

3. The eight travellers walked into the wooden house and saw

4. Yuba Bill held the stagecoach lamp near

5. Suddenly the Judge jumped and the others were frightened because

6. Bill went outside the house to

7. Miggles ran after the stagecoach for a mile because

C. Clauses with *who* and *which*

Put the two sentences together, using the words *who* or *which*.

Example:

The Judge liked to talk. He slept with his mouth open.

The Judge, who liked to talk, slept with his mouth open.

1. The lady from Virginia City wore expensive clothes. She was asleep, too.

2. The man on horseback was a stranger. He lifted his hand in goodbye.

3. The road got worse and wetter. It led to Miggles's house.

4. The voice sounded high and strange. It came from the house.

5. The man was sitting near the fire. He didn't speak.

6. The fire burned brightly. It warmed the cold travellers.

7. Miggles was lovely and young. She came in wet from the outside.

Note: Exercises D and E are about Part II (pp. 49–52).

D. Question Asking

Make questions for the following answers. You can make more than one question for each answer.

Example:

Coffee, bread, and some meat.

What did they have for dinner?
        or
What did Miggles give them to eat?

1. Joaquin.

2. They didn't like her very much.

3. In low voices, quickly, all together.

4. In '53.

5. They thought Jim would die.

6. Because she loved him.

7. She did not like goodbyes.

8. "Let's drink to Miggles!"

E. Skeleton Sentences

Make complete sentences from the following words. Use the correct form of the verb that is given. Add other necessary words like *the, a, an, with, on, her,* etc.

Example:

"Who / help me / dinner?" she said.

"Who will help me with the dinner?" she said.

1. The bear / stand up / two legs / like / man.

2. Pictures / walls / Miggles's house / be / newspapers.

3. Miggles / turn / eyes / the fire / and / not speak.

4. Miggles / own / Polka Bar / Marysville / '53.

5. "Why / you / not marry / Jim?" asked the Judge. "You give / young life."

6. Morning / coffee / table / Miggles / not be / there.

7. Men / drink / Miggles / resting place.

F. Writing:
The Lady from Virginia City

In this exercise, you are the Lady from Virginia City. You don't like Miggles. After the stagecoach trip is finished, you decide to write a letter to your friend, the Judge. You want to tell him *why* you don't like Miggles. Begin your letter with the words "My dear Judge." Sign your name after the words "Sincerely yours."

In your letter you might want to answer some or all of the following questions:

What are you writing to the Judge about?

Have you ever met a woman like Miggles before?

Does she seem like a lady to you, or not?

How does she dress?

Where does she live?

What does she have on her walls?

Who lives with her? Are they married? What do you think of that?

Who else lives with them?

What do you remember about Marysville in '53? What did Miggles do there?

Did she have a good name or a bad name?

Did people think she was wild, or quiet?

What did the Judge do at the resting place?

Do you understand why he said nice things about Miggles?

What did the French lady think about Miggles? Do you agree with her?

What do you think Miggles should do?

A
CUB-PILOT'S
EDUCATION

adapted from the story by

Mark Twain

Mark Twain's real name was Samuel Langhorne Clemens. He was born in 1835 in Missouri. As a boy, he lived in a small town on the Mississippi River. His most famous books, *The Adventures of Tom Sawyer* and *The Adventures of Huckleberry Finn,* are about boyhood and the Mississippi. Because of these books, Mark Twain became America's most famous and best-loved writer. He died in 1910 at the age of seventy-five. The following story is from his book *Life on the Mississippi.*

I

All the boys in my village wanted to be the same thing: a steamboat pilot. Our village lay on the great Mississippi River. Once a day, at noon, a steamboat came up from St. Louis. Later, at 1:00 o'clock, another came down from Keokuk. Before these hours, the day was full and bright with waiting. After them, the day was a dead and empty thing.

I can see that old time now. The white town sleeps in the morning sun. The streets are empty. Some animals walk near the buildings. The waters of the Mississippi are quiet and still. A man who has drunk too much lies peacefully near the river. Other men sit outside their stores in chairs. They look at the town and don't talk much.

Then a worker cries, "S-t-e-a-m-boat coming!" And everything changes! The man who has drunk too much gets up and runs. Suddenly the streets are full. Men, women, and children run to the steamboat landing. The animals make a hundred different noises. The town wakes up!

The steamboat which comes toward the town is long and pretty. Her big wheel turns and turns. Everybody looks at her and at the men who live on her. The pilot stands tallest, the center of everything, the king. Slowly the steamboat comes to the landing. Men take things off the boat and bring other things on. In ten minutes she is gone again. The town goes back to sleep. But the boys of the town remember the boat. They remember the pilot. And they don't forget.

I was fifteen then, and I ran away from home. I went to New Orleans. There I met a pilot named Mr. Bixby. I said I wanted to be his cub-pilot, or learner. He said no—but only

once. I said yes a hundred times. So in the end I won. He said he would teach me the river. He didn't smile or laugh, but I was the happiest boy in that city.

We left New Orleans at four o'clock one afternoon. Mr. Bixby was at the wheel. Here at the beginning of the river, there were a lot of steamboats. Most of them were at landings on the sides of the river. We went past them quickly, very close to them. Suddenly Mr. Bixby said, "Here. You steer her." And he gave me the wheel. My heart was in my mouth. I thought it was very dangerous, close to those other boats. I began to steer into the middle of the river. In the middle, there was enough water for everybody.

"What are you doing?" Mr. Bixby cried angrily. He pushed me away and took the wheel again. And again he steered us near the other boats. After a while, he became a little cooler. He told me that water runs fast in the middle of a river. At the sides, it runs slow. "So if you're going up-river, you have to steer near the sides. You can go in the middle only if you're going down-river." Well, that was good enough for me. I decided to be a down-river pilot only.

Sometimes Mr. Bixby showed me points of land. "This is Six-Mile Point," he said. The land pointed like a finger into the water. Another time, he said, "This is Nine-Mile Point." It looked like Six-Mile Point to me. Later, he said, "This is Twelve-Mile Point." Well, this wasn't very interesting news. All the points seemed the same.

After six hours of this, we had supper and went to bed. Even bed was more interesting than the "points." At midnight, someone put a light in my eyes. "Hey, let's go!"

Then he left. I couldn't understand this. I decided to go back to sleep. Soon the man came again with his light; now he was angry. "Wake up!" he called. I was angry, too, and said, "Don't put that light in my eyes! How can I sleep if you wake me up every minute?"

All the men in the room laughed at this. The man left

again, but came back soon with Mr. Bixby. One minute later I was climbing the steps to the pilot-house. Some of my clothes were on me. The rest were in my hands. Mr. Bixby walked behind me, angry. Now, here was something interesting: Pilots worked in the middle of the night!

And that night was a bad one. There was a lot of mist on the river. You could not see through it. Where were we going? I was frightened. But Mr. Bixby turned the wheel easily and happily. He told me we had to find a farm. Jones Farm. To myself I said, "Okay, Mr. Bixby. You can try all night. But you'll never find anything in this mist."

Suddenly Mr. Bixby turned to me and said, "What's the name of the first point above New Orleans?"

I answered very quickly. I said I didn't know.

"Don't *know*?"

The loudness of his voice surprised me. But I couldn't answer him.

"Well, then," he said, "What's the name of the next point?"

Again I didn't know.

"Now, look! After Twelve-Mile Point, where do you cross the river?"

"I-I-I don't know."

"You-you-you don't know? Well, what *do* you know?"

"I—nothing, it seems."

"Nothing? *Less* than nothing! You say you want to pilot a steamboat on the river? My boy, you couldn't pilot a cow down a street! Why do you think I told you the names of those points?"

"Well, to-to—be interesting, I thought."

"What?! To be *interesting*?" Now he was *very* angry. He walked across the pilot-house and back again. This cooled him down. "My boy," he said more softly, "You must get a little notebook. I will tell you many names of places on this river. You must write them all down. Then you must remember them. All of them. That is the only way to become a pilot."

My heart fell. I never remembered things easily in school. But also I didn't fully believe Mr. Bixby. No one, I thought, could know all of the Mississippi. No one could put that great river inside his head.

Then Mr. Bixby pulled a bell. A worker's voice came up from below.

"What's this, sir?"

"Jones Farm," Mr. Bixby said.

I could see nothing through the mist. And Mr. Bixby could see nothing. I knew that. So I didn't believe him. How could I? We were in the middle of nowhere! But soon the boat's nose softly hit the landing. Workers' voices came up to us. I still couldn't believe it, but this was Jones Farm!

II

And so, slowly, I began to put the Mississippi River inside my head. I filled a notebook—I filled two notebooks—with names from the river. Islands, towns, points, bends in the river. The names of all these things went into my notebooks. And slowly some of them began to go into my head. Then more of them. I began to feel better about myself. I was beginning to learn the river.

Then one day Mr. Bixby said to me, "What is the shape of Apple Bend?"

"The shape of Apple Bend?"

"Yes, of course."

"I know the *name* of Apple Bend. I know where it is. Don't tell me I have to know the shape of it, too!"

Mr. Bixby's mouth went off like a gun, bang! He shot all his bad words at me. Then, as always, he cooled. "My boy," he said, "You must learn the shape of this river and everything on it. If you don't know the shape, you can't steer at night. And of course the river has two shapes. One during the day, and one at night."

"Oh, no!"

"Oh, yes. Look: How can you walk through a room at home in the dark? Because you know the shape of it. You can't *see* it."

"You mean I must know this river like the rooms at home?"

"No. I mean you must know it *better* than the rooms at home."

"I want to die."

"My boy, I don't want you to be sad or angry. But there is more."

"All right. Tell me everything. Give it to me!"

"I'm sorry, but you must learn these things. There is no other way. Now, a night with stars throws shadows. Dark shadows change the shape of the river. You think you are coming to a bend, but there *is* no bend. And this is different from a night with no stars. On a night with no stars, the river has a different shape. You think there are no bends, but there *are* bends. And of course, on a night with mist, the river has *no* shape. You think you are going to steer the boat onto land. But then suddenly you see that it's water, not land. Well. Then you have your moonlight nights. Different kinds of moonlight change the shape of the river again. And there are different kinds of shadows, too. Different shadows bring different shapes to the river. You see——"

"Oh, stop!" I cried. "You mean I have to learn the thousand million different shapes of this river?"

"No, no! You only learn *the* shape of the river. The *one* shape. And you steer by that. Don't you understand? You steer by the river that's in your head. Forget the one that's before your eyes."

"I see. And you think that's easy."

"I never said it was easy. And of course the river is always, always changing shape. The river of this week is different from the river of last week. And next week it will be different again."

"All right. Goodbye. I'm going home."

But of course I didn't go home. I stayed. I wanted to learn. I *needed* to learn. And day by day, month by month, I did learn. The river was my school. Slowly I began to think I was a good student. I could steer the boat alone, without Mr. Bixby's help. I knew the river like the rooms of my house— no, better. I could steer at night, by the shape of the river in my head. No cub-pilot was better, I thought. Oh, my nose was very high in the air!

Of course, Mr. Bixby saw this. And he decided to teach me another lesson.

One beautiful summer's day we were near the bend above Island 66. I had the wheel. We were in the middle of the river. It was easy water, deep and wide.

Mr. Bixby said, "I am going below for a while. Do you know how to run the next bend?"

A strange question! It was perhaps the easiest bend in the river. I knew it well. It began at a little island. The river was wide there, and more than a hundred feet deep. There was no possible danger.

"Know how to *run* it? Why, I can run it with my eyes closed!"

"How much water is there in it?"

"What kind of question is that? There's more water there than in the Atlantic Ocean."

"You think so, do you?"

He left, and soon I began to worry. There was something in his voice. . . .

I didn't know it, but Mr. Bixby had stayed close to the pilot-house. I couldn't see him, but he was talking to some of the men. Soon a worker came and stood in front of the pilot-house. He looked a little worried. We were near the island at the beginning of the bend. Another man came and stood with the first. He looked worried, too. Then another. They looked at me, then at the water, then at me again. Soon there were fifteen or twenty people out there in front of me. No one said anything. The noise of the engines suddenly seemed loud to me.

Then one of them said in a strange voice, "Where is Mr. Bixby?"

"Below," I said. The man turned away and said nothing more.

Now I became *very* worried. I steered a little to the right. I thought I saw danger! I steered to the left. More danger! I wanted to go slower. I wanted to stop the engines. I didn't know *what* I wanted.

In the end I called down to the engine room. "How deep is it here? Can you tell me soon? Please be quick!"

"Forty feet," came the voice. He had the answer already! Forty feet? It couldn't be! Why, the water there was as deep as. . . .

"Thirty-five," he said in a worried voice. "Thirty-two! Twenty-eight!"

I couldn't believe it! I ran to the wheel, pulled a bell, stopped the engines.

"Eighteen!" came the voice. "Fifteen! Thirteen! Ten!"

Ten feet! I was filled with fear now. I did not know what to do. I called loudly down to the man in the engine room. "Back!" I called. "Please, Ben, back her! Back her! Oh, Ben, if you love me, back her now!"

I heard the door close softly. I looked around, and there stood Mr. Bixby. He smiled a sweet smile at me. Then all the people in front of the pilot-house began to laugh. I understood it all now, and I felt two feet tall. I started the engines again. I steered to the middle of the river without

another word. After a while, I said, "That was kind and loving of you, *wasn't* it? I think I'll hear that story the rest of my life."

"Well, perhaps you will. And that won't be a bad thing. I want you to learn something from this. Didn't you *know* there was a hundred feet of water at that bend?"

"Yes, I did."

"All right, then. If you know a thing, you must believe it—and deeply. The river is in your head, remember? And another thing. If you get into a dangerous place, don't turn and run. That doesn't help. You must fight fear, always. And on the river there is always fear."

It was a good lesson, perhaps his best lesson. And I never forgot it. But I can tell you, it cost a lot to learn it. Every day for weeks and weeks I had to hear those difficult words: "Oh, Ben, if you love me, back her!"

EXERCISES

A. Reading Skill:
Scanning Different Sources of Information

For this exercise you will need to use the paragraphs about Edgar Allan Poe (p. 13), Bret Harte (p. 43), and Mark Twain (p. 61). Scan those paragraphs to find answers to the questions below.

1. Which of the three writers lived the longest life? Which lived the shortest life?

2. Which writer was born in the Midwest?

3. Which writer was born in the East and moved to the far West?

4. Which writer died in London?

5. Which writer is famous for his detective stories?

6. Which writer worked for the U.S. government?

7. Which writer died poor and unhappy?

B. Reading Skill:
Analyzing Ideas Through Close Reading

Note: Questions 1–6 are about Part I (pp. 62–67). Questions 7–12 are about Part II (pp. 67–72). The other exercises draw on the whole story.

Read the sentence from the story. Then answer the question about the sentence.

1. "All the boys in my village wanted to be the same thing: A steamboat pilot." (p. 62)
   Why did all the boys want this?

2. "Then a worker cries, 'S-t-e-a-m-boat coming!' And everything changes!" (p. 62)
   What were some of these changes?

3. "So in the end I won." (p. 65)
   What did the boy win? How did he win it?

4. "I began to steer into the middle of the river." (p. 65)
   Why did the boy do this?

5. "Well, that was good enough for me. I decided to be a down-river pilot only." (p. 65)
   Why did the boy decide this? Why was it easier to steer down-river than up-river?

6. "My heart fell." (p. 67)
   What does this mean? Why did it happen?

7. "And so, slowly, I began to put the Mississippi River inside my head." (p. 67)
   What made the boy decide to do this? How did he do it?

8. "'You steer by the river that's in your head. Forget the one that's before your eyes.'" (p. 68)
   Did Mr. Bixby say this about daytime steering or nighttime steering? Why?

9. "Oh, my nose was very high in the air!" (p. 69)
   Why did the boy feel so good about himself?

10. "'Eighteen!' came the voice. 'Fifteen! Thirteen! Ten!'" (p. 70)
    Why did these numbers frighten the boy? Why did they surprise him?

11. "I understood it all now, and I felt two feet tall." (p. 70)
What did the boy understand? Why did he feel so small?

12. "It was a good lesson, perhaps his best lesson." (p. 72)
What are some things the boy learned from this lesson?

C. Word Forms

To the left of each sentence below is a word. Put the correct form of this word in the empty space in the sentence.

Example:

(kind) They showed me a lot of _____ *kindness* _____ at their home.

1. (peaceful) The man who has drunk too much lies _____ near the river.

2. (point) In some places, the land _____ like a finger into the river.

3. (worry) The men in front of the pilot-house had _____ faces.

4. (cool) He was very angry at first, but after a while he

_____.

5. (danger) The river can be very _____ when it is covered with mist.

6. (back) At noon, the pilot steered the boat to the landing. After twenty minutes, he _____ her away again.

7. (loud) The _____ of his voice surprised the boy.

8. (easy) It was the _____ bend in the river.

9. (begin) We were near the island at the _____ of the bend.

10. (interest) I didn't tell you those things just to be _____.

D. Crossword Puzzle

Find the word which explains or completes the sentence, or answers the question. Write the word in the right boxes, one letter for each box. Some words go across, some down. The first letter of each word is given. Number 1 Across has been done for you.

Across

1. One way to travel down the Mississippi River   (S)

2. If you don't know the _____ of the river, you can't find your way at night.   (S)

3. Mr. Bixby   (P)

4. The boy turned it to the left and to the right.   (W)

5. "Why do you think I told you the names of all those points? To be _____?"   (I)

Down

1. It can change the shape of the river. ·(S)

2. Mr. Bixby would usually get _____ before he got cool.   (H)

3. What did the boy begin to do with the boat on his first day as cub-pilot?   (S)

4. What was the boy in, when Mr. Bixby got him at midnight?   (B)

5. The nose of the boat softly touched the _____ at Jones Farm.   (L)

6. No one could see through the _____ on the river.   (M)

E. Connectors

For each empty space in the sentences below, choose the correct connector from the list. Each connector can be used only once.

before   because   when

so   after   then

                        but

1. The boy ran away from home _____ he
   wanted to be a steamboat pilot.

2. He wanted to be a steamboat pilot _____
   he knew about the hard work on the job.

3. All the points seemed the same to the boy,
   _____ he didn't remember them.

4. Mr. Bixby usually cooled _____ he got
   angry.

5. No one could see through the mist, _____
   Bixby found Jones Farm.

6. First he learned the names of the points and bends on the
   river, _____ he had to remember their different shapes.

7. The boy began to worry _____ he was
   alone in the pilot-house.

F. Writing:
Mr. Bixby and Ben Make Plans

In the story, Ben is the man in the engine room. When the
boy calls down to him to ask how deep the water is, he
answers "forty feet"—but really the water is much deeper

than that. Mr. Bixby has made a plan with Ben to fool the boy.

Write a dialogue between Ben and Mr. Bixby. In your dialogue, show how they made their plan. What do they say, exactly, when they decide that

- they will teach the young cub a lesson
- they will make him think that the deep water is not deep
- they will leave him alone in the pilot-house
- they will tell the other workers to come and stand in front of the pilot-house and look worried
- the boy will get worried
- one of the workers will ask for Mr. Bixby
- the boy will get even more worried
- he will try to steer away from danger
- he will call down to the engine room to find how deep the water is
- Ben will say "forty feet" at first—then less and less
- the boy will try to stop the boat
- then he . . .
- then . . .

THE LADY,
OR THE TIGER?

adapted from the story by

Frank Stockton

Frank R. Stockton was born in 1834. His most famous stories are in the form of fairy tales, ghost stories, or romances. But in all of them his humor has an edge like a knife. When "The Lady, or the Tiger?" was published in *Century Magazine* in 1882, it caused excitement all over the country. Hundreds of people wrote letters to the magazine or to their newspapers about it. Many letters demanded an answer to the question which the story asks. Others asked if the story was really about government, or psychology, or the battle of the sexes, or something else. Wisely, Stockton never answered any of the letters. The story remains as fresh today as it was then. Frank Stockton died in 1902.

Before you read this story, do Exercise A on p. 89.

A long, long time ago, there was a semi-barbaric king. I call him semi-barbaric because the modern world, with its modern ideas, had softened his barbarism a little. But still, his ideas were large, wild, and free. He had a wonderful imagination. Since he was also a king of the greatest powers, he easily turned the dreams of his imagination into facts. He greatly enjoyed talking to himself about ideas. And, when he and himself agreed upon a thing, the thing was done. He was a very pleasant man when everything in his world moved smoothly. And when something went wrong, he became even more pleasant. Nothing, you see, pleased him more than making wrong things right.

One of this semi-barbaric king's modern ideas was the idea of a large arena. In this arena, his people could watch both men and animals in acts of bravery.

But even this modern idea was touched by the king's wild imagination. In his arena, the people saw more than soldiers fighting soldiers, or men fighting animals. They enjoyed more than the sight of blood. In the king's arena, the people saw the laws of the country at work. They saw good men lifted up and bad men pushed down. Most important, they were able to watch the workings of the first law of Chance.

Here is what happened when a man was accused of a crime. If the king was interested in the crime, then the people were told to come to the arena. They came together and sat there, thousands of them. The king sat high up in his king's chair. When he gave a sign, a door below him opened. The accused man stepped out into the arena. Across from him, on the other side of the arena, were two other doors. They were close together and they looked the same. The accused man would walk straight to these doors and open one of them. He could choose either one of the doors. He was forced by nothing and led by no one. Only Chance helped him—or didn't help him.

Behind one of the doors was a tiger. It was the wildest, biggest, hungriest tiger that could be found. Of course, it quickly jumped on the man. The man quickly—or not so quickly—died. After he died, sad bells rang, women cried, and the thousands of people walked home slowly.

But, if the accused man opened the other door, a lady would step out. She was the finest and most beautiful lady that could be found. At that moment, there in the arena, she would be married to the man. It didn't matter if the man was already married. It didn't matter if he was in love with another woman. The king did not let little things like that get in the way of his imagination. No, the two were married there in front of the king. There was music and dancing. Then happy bells rang, women cried, and the thousands of people walked home singing.

This was the way the law worked in the king's semi-barbaric country. Its fairness is clear. The criminal could not know which door the lady was behind. He opened either door as he wanted. At the moment he opened the door, he did not know if he was going to be eaten or married.

The people of the country thought the law was a good one. They went to the arena with great interest. They never knew if they would see a bloody killing or a lovely marriage. This uncertainty gave the day its fine and unusual taste. And they liked the fairness of the law. Wasn't it true that the accused man held his life in his own hands?

This semi-barbaric king had a daughter. The princess

was as beautiful as any flower in the king's imagination. She had a mind as wild and free as the king's. She had a heart like a volcano. The king loved her deeply, watched her closely, and was very jealous of her. But he could not always watch her. And in his castle lived a young man. This young man was a worker. He was a good worker, but he was of low birth. He was brave and beautiful, and the princess loved him, and was jealous of him. Because of the girl's semi-barbarism, her love was hot and strong. Of course, the young man quickly returned it. The lovers were happy together for many months. But one day the king discovered their love. Of course he did not lose a minute. He threw the young man into prison and named a day for his appearance in the arena.

There had never been a day as important as that one. The country was searched for the strongest, biggest, most dangerous tiger. With equal care, the country was searched for the finest and most beautiful young woman. There was no question, of course, that the young man had loved the princess. He knew it, she knew it, the king knew it, and everybody else knew it, too. But the king didn't let this stand in the way of his excellent law. Also, the king knew that the young man would now disappear from his daughter's life. He would disappear with the other beautiful lady. Or he would disappear into the hungry tiger. The only question was, "Which?"

And so the day arrived. Thousands and thousands of people came to the arena. The king was in his place, across from those two doors that seemed alike but were truly very different.

All was ready. The sign was given. The door below the king opened, and the lover of the princess walked into the arena. Tall, beautiful, fair, he seemed like a prince. The people had not known that such a fine young man had lived among them. Was it any wonder that the princess had loved him?

The young man came forward into the arena, and then turned towards the king's chair. But his eyes were not on the king. They were on the princess, who sat to her father's right. Perhaps it was wrong for the young lady to be there. But remember that she was still semi-barbaric. Her wild heart would not let her be away from her lover on this day. More important, she now knew the secret of the doors. Over the past few days, she had used all of her power in the castle, and much of her gold. She had discovered which door hid the tiger, and which door hid the lady.

She knew more than this. She knew the lady. It was one of the fairest and loveliest ladies in the castle. In fact, this lady was more than fair and lovely. She was thoughtful, kind, loving, full of laughter, and quick of mind. The princess hated her. She had seen, or imagined she had seen, the lady looking at the young man. She thought these looks had been noticed and even returned. Once or twice she had seen them talking together. Perhaps they had talked for only a moment. Perhaps they had talked of nothing important. But how could the princess be sure of that? The other girl was lovely and kind, yes. But she had lifted her eyes to the lover of the princess. And so, in her semi-barbaric heart, the princess was jealous, and hated her.

Now, in the arena, her lover turned and looked at her. His eyes met hers, and he saw at once that she knew the secret of the doors. He had been sure that she would know it. He understood her heart. He had known that she would try to learn this thing which no one else knew—not even the king. He had known she would try. And now, as he looked at her, he saw that she had succeeded.

At that moment, his quick and worried look asked the question: "Which?" This question in his eyes was as clear to

the princess as spoken words. There was no time to lose. The question had been asked in a second. It must be answered in a second.

Her right arm rested on the arm of her chair. She lifted her hand and made a quick movement towards the right. No one saw except her lover. Every eye except his was on the man in the arena.

He turned and walked quickly across the empty space. Every heart stopped beating. Every breath was held. Every eye was fixed upon that man. Without stopping for even a second, he went to the door on the right and opened it.

Now, the question is this: Did the tiger come out of that door, or did the lady?

As we think deeply about this question, it becomes harder and harder to answer. We must know the heart of the animal called man. And the heart is difficult to know. Think of it, dear reader, and remember that the decision is not yours. The decision belongs to that hot-blooded, semi-barbaric princess. Her heart was at a white heat beneath the fires of jealousy and painful sadness. She had lost him, but who should have him?

Very often, in her thoughts and in her dreams, she had cried out in fear. She had imagined her lover as he opened the door to the hungry tiger.

And even more often she had seen him at the other door! She had bitten her tongue and pulled her hair. She had hated his happiness when he opened the door to the lady. Her heart burned with pain and hatred when she imagined the scene: He goes quickly to meet the woman. He leads her into the arena. His eyes shine with new life. The happy bells ring wildly. The two of them are married before her eyes. Children run around them and throw flowers. There is music, and the thousands of people dance in the streets. And the princess's cry of sadness is lost in the sounds of happiness!

Wouldn't it be better for him to die at once? Couldn't he wait for her in the beautiful land of the semi-barbaric future?

But the tiger, those cries of pain, that blood!

Her decision had been shown in a second. But it had been made after days and nights of deep and painful thought. She had known she would be asked. She had decided what to answer. She had moved her hand to the right.

The question of her decision is not an easy one to think about. Certainly I am not the one person who should have to answer it. So I leave it with all of you: Which came out of the opened door—the lady, or the tiger?

EXERCISES

A. Reading Skill:
Skimming to Get an Impression

Read the paragraph about Frank Stockton on p. 81. Then skim the story of "The Lady, or the Tiger?" Read only the first sentence or two of each paragraph. Next, write down at least five sentences which explain the impression, or general idea which you have received from skimming the story. Do not re-read. Write only from memory. Try to answer some of the following questions.

When does the story take place?

What kind of people appear in the story?

How many people do you remember reading about?

Does the story seem to be "realistic"?

Does the story ask a question, or give an answer?

What, generally, does the story seem to be about?

What are a few interesting words that you remember reading?

Do you think you will enjoy reading the story? Why or why not?

Finally, compare your impressions with those of other students in your class.

B. Reading Skill:
Understanding Pronouns

In the following sentences, the word this, that, or it has been underlined. Find the sentence in the story (page and paragraph numbers are given). Then tell what words or ideas are meant by this, that, or it.

Examples:

(p. 84, paragraph 1) The young man quickly returned it. *"It" means: the princess's love.*

(p. 85, paragraph 2) She knew more than this. *"This" means: which door hid the tiger, and which door hid the lady.*

1. (p. 83, para 3) The king did not let little things like that get in the way of his imagination.

2. (p. 83, para 4) This was the way the law worked in the king's semi-barbaric country.

3. (p. 83, para 5) This uncertainty gave the day its fine and unusual taste. (What uncertainty?)

4. (p. 84, para 2) But the king didn't let this stand in the way of his excellent law.

5. (p. 85, para 2) But how could the princess be sure of that?

6. (p. 85, para 3) He had been sure that she would know it.

7. (p. 88, para 4) Certainly I am not the one person who should have to answer it.

C. Verb Tense

1. The following paragraph is from the story. Change it into the past tense. *Be careful:* the verbs are irregular.

He goes quickly to meet the woman. He leads her into the arena. His eyes shine with new life. The happy bells ring wildly. The two of them are married before her eyes. Children run around them and throw flowers.

2. The following paragraphs are also from the story. Change them back into the present tense. *Be careful:* you will have to use the future and present perfect tenses in addition to the present tense.

There had never been a day as important as that one. The country was searched for the strongest, biggest, most dangerous tiger. With equal care, the country was searched for the finest and most beautiful young woman. . . . The king knew that the young man would now disappear from his daughter's life. He would disappear with the other beautiful lady. Or he would disappear into the hungry tiger. The only question was, "Which?"

The princess hated her. She had seen, or imagined she had seen, the lady looking at the young man. She thought these looks had been noticed and even returned. Once or twice she had seen them talking together. Perhaps they had talked for only a moment. Perhaps they had talked of nothing important. But how could the princess be sure of that?

D. Vocabulary and Word Forms: Noun and Adjective

Below are a noun form and an adjective form of seven words from the story. Place each pair of words correctly in the sentence which best fits their meaning. *Be careful:* You may use each pair of words only once!

imagination–imaginative

barbarian–barbaric

accusation–accused

marriage–married

jealousy–jealous

decision–decisive

danger–dangerous

1. The king was a very _____ man; once he made a _____ about something, nothing could change his mind.

2. The king was also quite _____; only a wild, free _____ could think of using an arena to show the workings of the first law of Chance.

3. Of course, the arena was a _____ place for a criminal; the _____ was in the form of a tiger hidden behind one of the doors.

4. The _____ against a man might be wrong or unfair; still, the _____ person had to choose one of the doors and open it.

5. If a lady came out, a _____ was performed at once in the arena; and it didn't matter if the man was already _____.

6. If another woman loved the man, we can imagine that her _____ would be great; in fact, in that country, they said a _____ woman was as dangerous as a tiger.

7. Certainly, such ideas seem rather _____ to us; so, if we like the story, is that because the story pleases the _____in all of us?

E. Comparisons with *one of the . . .*

Change the following sentences by using the form: *one of the* + [adjective + *-est*] or [*most* + adjective] (for example: *one of the widest,* or *one of the most wonderful*). Add the words *in the country* to complete the meaning of the new sentence.

Example:

He was a tall, beautiful man.

He was one of the tallest, most beautiful men in the country.

1. The king had a wild, free, and barbaric imagination.

2. It was a big, hungry tiger.

3. She had a fine, excellent mind.

4. It was a strange and dangerous law.

5. The lady was fair, lovely, and thoughtful.

6. It was a difficult secret to discover.

7. It was a hard, painful decision to make.

F. Discussion: The Pictures

1. Look at the picture on p. 86, showing the king and his daughter sitting in the arena.

   a. What has happened up until this moment in the story? What is going to happen soon?

   b. Describe the king in detail. Tell about his position in the chair; the expression on his face; the "atmosphere" surrounding him.

2. Now look at the picture on p. 88. The princess's lover is about to open one of the doors. In this picture, he turns and takes a final look at the princess. She has told him with her hand to open the door on the right. But here is a final question. Remember, the lover knows that the princess knows which door hides the lady, and which door

hides the tiger! How well does the lover know the princess? Which door will he open *now*?

G. Writing: Three-Paragraph Composition

"Which came out of the opened door—the lady, or the tiger?"

Write down the above question. Then write a paragraph which begins with the sentence, "Perhaps it was the lady who came out." Give at least three reasons why the princess chose the lady for her lover to find.

Then write a second paragraph which begins, "On the other hand, perhaps it was the tiger." Give at least three reasons why the princess chose the tiger.

Then write a third paragraph which begins with the words, "Personally, I think . . ." Give your own choice. Which of the reasons which you have written is the most important to you? Why?

AN OCCURRENCE AT OWL CREEK BRIDGE

adapted from the story by

Ambrose Bierce

Ambrose Bierce was born in Ohio in 1842. He went to school, a military academy, for just one year. In 1864, during the Civil War between the North and the South, Bierce joined the Army. After the war he went to California. He wrote political pieces for newspapers. His first short story was published in 1871. That same year he married and went to live in London. After five years in London he returned to the United States. He worked for the Hearst Newspaper Company on the West Coast. He went to write about the Mexican War in 1914, where he disappeared in the fighting. "An Occurrence at Owl Creek Bridge" appeared in a collection of short stories *Tales of Soldiers and Civilians* in 1891. A second collection, *Can Such Things Be?*, was published in 1893.

I

A man stood upon a railroad bridge in northern Alabama. He looked down into the river below. The man's hands were tied behind his back. A rope circled his neck. The end of the long rope was tied to part of the wooden bridge above his head.

Next to the man stood two soldiers of the Northern army. A short distance away stood their captain. Two soldiers guarded each end of the bridge. On one bank of the river, other soldiers stood silently, facing the bridge. The two guards at each end of the bridge faced the banks of the river. None of the soldiers moved. The captain, too, stood silent. He watched the work of the two soldiers near him, but he made no sign. All of them were waiting silently for Death. Death is a visitor who must be met with respect. Even soldiers, who see so much death, must show respect to Death. And in the army, silence and stillness are signs of respect.

The man with the rope around his neck was going to be hanged. He was about thirty-five years old. He was not dressed like a soldier. He wore a well-fitting coat. His face was a fine one. He had a straight nose, strong mouth, and dark hair. His large eyes were grey, and looked kind. He did not seem like the sort of man to be hanged. Clearly he was not the usual sort of criminal. But the Army has laws for hanging many kinds of people. And gentlemen are not excused from hanging.

When the two soldiers were ready, they stepped away.

The captain faced the condemned man. They stood face to face on a piece of wood. The middle of the board rested against the edge of the bridge. When the captain stepped off the board, the piece of wood would fall down into the river. The condemned man would fall down after the board. Only the rope around his neck would stop him. He would be hanged by the neck until dead. The man's face had not been covered. His eyes were open. He looked down at the river below. He saw a small piece of wood floating along with the river. How slowly it moved! What a gentle river!

He closed his eyes and thought of his wife and children. Until now, other things had filled his mind: the water, painted gold by the sun . . . the soldiers . . . the floating wood. After a little while he heard a new sound. A strange metallic sound kept beating through the thoughts of his family. He wondered what it was. It sounded far away, and yet very close. It was as slow as a death-bell ringing. The sound came louder and louder. It seemed to cut into his brain like a knife. He was afraid he would cry out. But it was only his own watch making its little sound.

He opened his eyes. He saw again the water below him. "If I could free my hands," he thought, "I might throw off the rope. I could jump into the river. If I swam quickly underwater, I could escape the bullets. I would reach the river bank, run into the woods and go home. My home, thank God, is still safe from the Northern Army." These thoughts must be written in words here. But they passed as quickly as light through the condemned man's mind.

And then the captain stepped off the board.

II

The condemned man's name was Peyton Farquhar. He was a rich farmer, the last son in an old Alabama family. He owned slaves who worked on his farm. Like other Southern farmers, he believed that slaves were necessary to Southern farming. The Northern government had said that it was against the law to have slaves. Now, the North and the South were at war.

Certain work had kept Peyton Farquhar from joining the Southern Army at the beginning of the war. But he was at heart a soldier. He did everything he could to help the South. No job was too low, no adventure too dangerous. One evening, Farquhar and his wife were sitting in the garden. A soldier rode up to the house. He was dressed like other soldiers in the Southern Army. While Mrs. Farquhar went to get him a drink of water, the soldier spoke with Farquhar.

"The Northerners are rebuilding the railroads," the soldier said. "They are getting ready for another advance. They've reached Owl Creek Bridge. They've fixed the bridge and moved in a lot of soldiers. Anyone who attacks the railroad or tries to destroy the bridge will be hanged."

"How far is it to Owl Creek Bridge?" Farquhar asked.

"About thirty miles."

"Are there soldiers on this side of the bridge?"

"Only a few guards."

"Suppose that a man went around the guards?" Farquhar smiled. "What could he do to stop the advance?"

The soldier thought a moment. Then he said, "I was at the bridge a month ago. I saw a lot of wood that the river had washed against one end of the bridge. It's very dry now, and the wood would burn quickly and well."

The lady had now brought the water. The soldier drank. He thanked her, bowed to Farquhar, and rode away. An hour later, after nightfall, he passed Farquhar's farm again. He went North in the direction he had come from. He was a Northern soldier.

III

Peyton Farquhar fell down from the bridge. He lost consciousness. He was like one already dead. He was awakened—hours later, it seemed to him—by the great pain in his neck. Pain passed through his body like rivers of fire. He was conscious of a fullness in his head. He could not think. He could only feel. He was conscious of motion. He seemed to be falling through a red cloud. Then suddenly the light flew upward with the noise of a loud splash. A fearful noise was in his ears. All was cold and dark. The power of thought came back to him. He knew the rope had broken, and he had fallen into the river. The rope around his neck was cutting off the air. To die of hanging at the bottom of a river! No! Impossible! He opened his eyes in the darkness. He saw light far, far above him. He was still going down, for the light grew smaller and smaller. But then it grew brighter, and he knew he was coming back up to the top of the river. Now he felt sorry to be coming out of the water. He had been so comfortable. "To be hanged and drowned," he thought. "That is not so bad. But I do not want to be shot. No, I will not be shot. That's not fair!"

He was not conscious of his actions until he felt pain in his hands. Then he realized that he was trying to free his hands. At last the rope fell off. His arms floated upward; he could see his hands. He watched with interest. His hands were trying to untie the rope around his neck. They pulled off the rope and it floated away. "Put it back, put it back," he felt himself crying. His neck hurt badly. His mind was on fire, his heart beat wildly enough to leave his body. His whole body was in great pain. But his hands pushed him up out of the water. And he took a great breath of air.

Now he was fully conscious. His five senses seemed unusually clear. The pain his body had felt made him see and feel the beauty around him. He felt the water against his skin. He heard the soft sound as it hit his neck and shoulders. He looked into the forest on the bank and could see each tree, each leaf. He could even see small forest animals between the trees. A fish swam before his eyes. He noticed how the sunlight shone on the fish's silver skin.

He was facing away from the bridge when his head came out of the water. Now he turned around. He saw small men on the bridge, dark against the blue sky. They cried out and pointed at him. The captain took out his gun but did not shoot.

Then, suddenly, he heard a loud bang. Something hit the water near his head. Water splashed in his face. He heard a second shot and a light blue cloud rose from the gun. Then Farquhar heard the captain call to the men: "Ready, men . . . Shoot!"

Farquhar swam deep under the water. The water sounded loud in his ears. But even above the sound of the water he heard the shots. He swam down the river.

Later he swam to the top again. He saw he was quite far from the bridge. The soldiers were still pointing their guns at him.

"The captain will not order them to shoot together again," he thought. "It's as easy to escape many bullets as one. He'll order them to shoot as they wish. God help me, I cannot escape them all."

Suddenly he was caught by a strong current in the river. The current pulled him under the water. It carried him down the river and turned him over and over. At last the force of the current pushed him up onto the bank.

He lay on the bank, crying with happiness and tiredness. He dug his fingers into the river bank. The small stones felt like jewels. The trees looked to him like a forest of gold. The air smelled clear and sweet, and a pink light shone through the trees.

The sound of bullets in the trees awoke him. He rose to his feet, frightened again, and disappeared into the forest.

All that day he traveled. The forest seemed endless. He could find no road. He hadn't realized before now that he lived near such a wild place.

When night began to fall, he was very tired and hungry. The thought of his wife and children helped him to continue. At last he found a road that seemed to lead in the right direction. It was as wide and straight as a city street. But it seemed untraveled. There were no fields, no houses nearby. The big black trees formed a straight wall on both sides. Overhead, great golden stars shone in the sky. The stars looked unfamiliar. He was sure that they were grouped in some strange order which meant bad luck. From inside the forest came strange noises. Among them he heard people talking in an unknown language.

His neck was in pain. He knew that the rope had left a black circle on his skin. He could not close his eyes. His tongue was dry; he felt very thirsty. Grass seemed to cover the road now; it was soft under his feet.

Did he fall asleep while he was walking? Now he sees something else. Perhaps he was wakened from a dream. Now he stands not far from the door of his own house. Everything looks just as he left it, bright and beautiful in the morning sunshine. He must have traveled through the whole night. As he walks toward the door, his wife appears to meet him. She stands waiting, cool and sweet, silent and still. She holds out her arms to him with a smile of happiness. Ah! how beautiful she is! He moves toward her with open arms. He moves slowly, closer, closer. At the moment he touches her, he feels a great pain at the back of his neck. A white light flames all about him. . . .

There was a loud bang, then silence. All was darkness . . .

Peyton Farquhar was dead. His body, with a broken
neck, hung from a rope beneath Owl Creek Bridge.

EXERCISES

*Note: Exercise A refers to the paragraph on p. 97. The
other exercises are divided into three parts, just as the story
is.*

A. Reading Skill:
Scanning for Specific Information

You are asked to find Ambrose Bierce's age, in years, at
some of the major events in his interesting life. To the left
of each statement below, write Bierce's age at the time
the event took place. To do this, you will have to scan the
paragraph about Bierce on p. 97, and make calculations
based on the information you find.

_____ Bierce joins the army.

_____ His first short story is published.

_____ He goes with his wife to London.

_____ He returns to the United States.

_____ He disappears in the Mexican War.

_____ "An Occurrence at Owl Creek Bridge" is published in a collection of stories.

Part I (pp. 98–101)

B. Reading Skill: Understanding the Setting

Answer the following questions with complete sentences.

1. Where was the man standing?

2. Why was there a rope around his neck?

3. Why were all the soldiers so silent?

4. Describe the man's clothes and face. What kind of a man did he seem to be?

5. What would happen when the captain stepped off one end of the board?

6. What sounded so loud to the man?

7. List five things that the man thought about while he was standing on the board. How quickly did he think about these things?

8. Look at the picture on p. 100. Describe the picture, using some or all of the following words: *above, below, over, under, high, in front of, face to face, captain, river, sword, to the side, board.*

C. Passive Voice

The following sentences mention things that were done to the man by the soldiers. Rewrite the sentences using the passive voice. It is not necessary to end each new sentence with the words "by the soldiers."

Example:
The soldiers tied the man's hands behind his back.

The man's hands were tied behind his back.

1. The soldiers circled the man's neck with a rope.
2. The soldiers were going to hang the man.
3. Soldiers do not excuse gentlemen from hanging.
4. The soldiers had not covered the man's face.
5. The soldiers were not destroying the man's home.

Part II (pp. 101–102)

D. Understanding Adverbial Clauses

Finish the sentence with clause **a, b, c,** or **d.**

1. Peyton Farquhar owned slaves
   a. until he understood that it was against the law.
   b. before he was a rich farmer.
   c. because he thought the South needed slaves.
   d. while the slaves wanted to work for him.

2. A Northern soldier came to Farquhar's house

    a. because he knew that Farquhar had helped the South in the war.

    b. before Farquhar had helped the South in the war.

    c. since the adventure was too dangerous.

    d. when he learned that the North and South were at war.

3. Farquhar decided to try to burn the bridge

    a. while the Northerners were rebuilding the railroads.

    b. before the Northerners fixed the bridge and moved in some soldiers.

    c. because Owl Creek Bridge was thirty miles from his home.

    d. after the soldier told him about the dry wood.

4. The soldier rode north

    a. until night came.

    b. before Mrs. Farquhar could bring him a drink of water.

    c. because he wanted to tell the Northern army about Farquhar.

    d. since he wanted to attack the Northern army.

E. Reported Speech

Change the following sentences to reported speech.

Example:

"Is it far to Owl Creek Bridge?" Farquhar asked.

Farquhar asked if it was far to Owl Creek Bridge.

1. "It's about thirty miles," the soldier told him.

2. "Are there soldiers on the south side of the bridge?" Farquhar wanted to know.

3. "There are only a few guards," the soldier said.

4. "Could a man go around the guards?" Farquhar wondered.

5. "I don't know how I could stop the advance," he added.

6. "I saw a lot of wood that the river washed against the bridge," the soldier explained.

Part III (pp. 103–106)

F. Reading Skill: The "Real" Meaning

If the sentence is true, write "T" beside it. If it is not true, write "F," for false, and then make a true sentence.

1. _____ After Farquhar fell from the bridge, the rope around his neck really broke.

2. _____ In his mind, for a second or two, Farquhar believed the rope had broken.

3. _____ Farquhar believed that his free hands tied the rope tighter around his neck underwater.

4. _____ Farquhar believed that the river current pushed him down and drowned him.

5. _____ Farquhar thought that he heard people talking in an unknown language in the forest.

6. _____ The bang which Farquhar heard at the end of the story was the sound of the soldiers shooting him.

7. _____ It took an hour or two for Farquhar's escape and adventure to pass through his mind.

8. _____ Nothing that happens to Farquhar in Part III is strange or unrealistic.

G. Making Questions

Make questions for the following answers. There are several possible questions for each answer.

Example:

Farquhar felt that it was unfair to be shot.

How did Farquhar feel about being shot?

   or

What did Farquhar feel was unfair?

1. Underwater, Farquhar freed his hands and untied the rope.

2. His five senses seemed unusually clear.

3. He called, "Ready, men . . . Shoot!"

4. He disappeared into the forest after he left the river.

5. His wife appeared to meet him at the door.

6. The escape had taken place in his mind.

H. Writing: Word Order and Controlled Composition

The words in the following sentences are in the wrong order. Put them in the correct order. Then put the sentences in correct order so that they tell a summary of the story of "An Occurrence at Owl Creek Bridge." Word groups are underlined.

Example:

during   takes place   the story   the Civil War

The story takes place during the Civil War.

1. into the river   that   to safety   he thought and swam   he fell

2. the Southern army   he tried   in the war to help

3. Southern farmer   was   a rich   Peyton Farquhar

4. he died   in fact   was   and   the escape from hanging   in his mind   however

5. he was falling   he dreamed   from the bridge while   of escaping

6. caught him   hanged him   the Northern army and   from Owl Creek Bridge

NOTES

NOTES

NOTES

NOTES

NOTES

NOTES